BASSOON TECHNIQUE

THE BASSOON IN PLAYING POSITION

Demonstrated by the author.

Bassoon Technique

BY

ARCHIE CAMDEN

London

OXFORD UNIVERSITY PRESS

New York   *Toronto*

Oxford University Press, Ely House, London W.1.

GLASGOW NEW YORK TORONTO MELBOURNE WELLINGTON
CAPE TOWN IBADAN NAIROBI DAR ES SALAAM LUSAKA ADDIS ABABA
DELHI BOMBAY CALCUTTA MADRAS KARACHI LAHORE DACCA
KUALA LUMPUR SINGAPORE HONG KONG TOKYO

ISBN 0 19 318606 3

© Oxford University Press, 1962

First published 1962
Reprinted 1965, 1972 and 1975

*Printed in Great Britain by
Chapel River Press, Andover, Hants.*

PREFACE

'The Woodwind is by far the most important section of the Orchestra. The Strings being merely "padding" and the Brass and Percussion merely "punctuation". And of the Woodwind group the Bassoon is the most attractive member.' So began the speaker at a Royal College of Music lecture some years ago. I know this was said—because I said it myself!

Having established the true position of the bassoon I want to explain the function of this book.

It does not aim at replacing the teacher. Discussion and criticism, demonstration and listening, will always be preferable to the written word. But frequently students and amateurs are so domiciled that it is impossible for them to get regular tuition, or even any tuition at all. It is hoped that these will derive help from these pages in their efforts towards understanding, and playing, the bassoon.

For those fortunate enough to have good, regular tuition, there may be something in this book to supplement their teaching, and provide additional interest, for it deals with the basic technique of the bassoon, as practised and taught by the author during a long musical life of bassooning.

I make no apologies for starting at the very beginning. Those who are well acquainted with the early days can skip at will.

Archie Camden

ACKNOWLEDGEMENTS

Acknowledgement is due to Boosey & Hawkes Music Publishers Ltd. for permission to quote an extract from Stravinsky's ' *Rite of Spring* '.

CONTENTS

ILLUSTRATIONS

THE INSTRUMENT

It is very important to start with a good instrument. It is never satisfactory to take the view that an old, poor instrument will do to start on, and a better one can be bought if you 'take to it and get on well'. It is not always realized that a poor instrument can have defects impossible to overcome even by an experienced player, let alone the beginner, who, in his initial frustration, may well decide the bassoon is not for him and then find he cannot even sell it. A good instrument is a joy to play on at all times, keeps its value, and gives the right assistance to the beginner. Expert advice should always be taken, and great care shown, before the purchase of an instrument, as there are many pitfalls. High pitch old bassoons, which have been converted to low pitch by the addition of small pieces of tubing and the re-boring of certain holes, are sometimes offered for sale, but they are rarely satisfactory. Also, bassoons with fundamental faults of intonation impossible to correct are sometimes offered at a tempting price. On the other hand certain faults of intonation can be corrected by an adjustment to the height of the pads, or by making some holes slightly larger or smaller. These matters can only be decided by an expert.

There are two types of bassoons—German and French.

Some 150 years ago steps were taken in both Germany and France to improve the bassoon, which until then had been a very capricious instrument with limited capabilities. These developments proceeded along entirely different lines, and eventually instruments differing in many important respects were produced. Only the French bassoon was used in England up to recent times. I think I was the first British player to use a German-type instrument. Now, however, this is the type generally used in this country, only a very few professional players still playing on the French type. Many of the fingerings differ between the German and French instruments, particularly those of the higher notes. The normal tone of the French bassoon is thin, reedy, and rather nasal, and the different quality of tone between high, middle, and low registers is marked. The normal tone of the German bassoon is full, round, and even throughout. From this it will be seen that I strongly recommend a German type instrument, though I always feel that, when played by a really fine artist, the French instrument sometimes sounds almost like a German one. The following are some of the makers of German bassoons: Heckel, Mönnig, Mollenhauer, Adler, Kohlert, and Schreiber. The instrument illustrated is by Mönnig.

Care of the instrument

The bassoon has five main parts (see plate II). Starting from the reed these are known as (a) the crook, (b) the tenor joint, (c) the double joint (or boot), (d) the long joint, and (e) the bell. There is also a small hand rest (f). Always put the instrument away after use. Never leave it standing in a corner, particularly on a polished floor, as it may slip down with disastrous results. Take it to pieces and always mop out the tenor joint and the narrow tube in the double joint, as this is where moisture will be found. I use a 'pull-through' for the tenor joint, as this avoids any possibility of wear at the narrow end of it.

The ends of the joints, where they fit together, are lapped with cork or cord, and should be kept slightly greased with vaseline or something similar. In damp weather the lapped ends swell slightly and are sometimes inclined to stick. At these times be more free with the vaseline. In dry weather they may become loose; if the shrinking is excessive and causes a leak, wet the cork to make it swell and pass a lighted match or taper lightly over the cork.

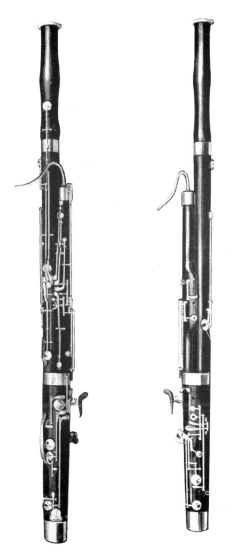

Plate I. THE BASSOON

Front and back views.

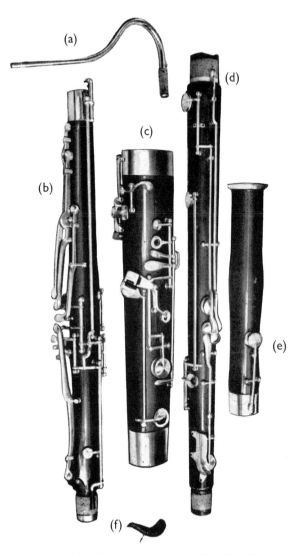

(a)

(d)

(c)

(b)

(e)

(f)

Plate II. PARTS OF THE INSTRUMENT

For details see page 2.

In the keywork, attention should be given regularly to the springs, moving parts, rods, and so forth. Use only the best machine oil which can be applied to the springs with a fine paintbrush, and to the rods and moving parts with a needle. If a spring should break, a rubber band will usually make a temporary substitute.

Pads must be watched carefully to ensure they do not leak. Even a slight leak will make the instrument hard to blow, while a large one will also affect the intonation. If I suspect a pad I test it with a strip of cigarette paper cut like a wedge. I insert the tapered end underneath the pad and close it firmly—as though playing the note. If the wedge of paper can be easily pulled out *there* is the leak. Always renew a leaking pad at once. New pads can be bought and are easily fixed with shellac.

At intervals of a year or two it is advisable to give a slight oiling to the interior of the wooden tubes. These are the *larger* tube in the double joint, the long joint, and the bell. This should be done with almond oil, or other light vegetable oil, and an impregnated cloth should be used, taking care that no oil leaks on to the pads. The other joints, being ebonite lined, should never have oil in contact with the lining. It is as well to have the instrument overhauled once a year by a competent repairer.

The crook is a vital part of the instrument. Most bassoons have two crooks supplied with them, No. 1 being slightly shorter, and therefore sharper, than No. 2. The crook must be kept clean inside and there is a thin bristle brush for this supplied by instrument makers.

Should one of these crooks be lost or damaged experiment with a number of crooks as there is an infinite variety of them. Having found one that suits your particular instrument—and you—stick to it and get on with your practising There is far too much hankering after unobtainable perfection in regard to instruments and equipment on the part of some players. It is as well to accept the fact, here and now, that there is no such thing as the perfect bassoon, and that the job in hand is to learn how to play well on the best available.

FIRST STEPS—THE FOUNDATION OF TECHNIQUE

I am going to assume that you are a beginner, and I would first of all recommend strongly that you obtain good regular tuition. If this is not possible at least start with some good lessons. It is essential to be set on the right tracks at the beginning, then if you have to proceed on your own an occasional lesson will ensure that faults which may creep in are corrected before they become bad habits.

The teacher will see that the instrument is in good playing order and will advise on that thorny subject, the reed. I am going to deal with reeds in detail in a later chapter.

You have, therefore, an instrument and a reed, and also a sling to put round your neck which will take most of the weight of the bassoon. You should also have a fingering chart.

Stand straight up with the whole body relaxed, head erect, chest well out, and no suggestion of a stoop. It is advisable to do most of your practice standing. When you get to the stage of playing with others, I suggest you practise your part privately sitting down, and do not follow the example of one enthusiastic young man who, when playing chamber music with his friends, always stood up to play his more difficult passages because he had practised them that way at home and felt at a disadvantage sitting down—a habit that completely unnerved his colleagues and perplexed the onlookers!

When you do sit down to practise be careful to sit up straight. There are too many round-shouldered wind and string players about.

Hold the bassoon with the right hand on the hand rest (most German bassoons have this) and the left hand with fingers 1, 2 and 3 covering the three holes in the tenor joint. This will give C, a good firm note with which to start.

We must deal now with the embouchure. This is the word used to describe the position and shape of the lips necessary for the playing of wind instruments. An experienced player acquires an embouchure which, in shape and muscular tension, is suitable for playing his instrument. This will vary considerably from player to player, dependent on his physical characteristics—lip muscles, teeth formation, etc.—and takes time. The beginner's lips are always slack and uncontrollable, and in his endeavour to carry out instructions he will find they tire quickly at first. For this reason alone it is recommended that practice should only occupy a few minutes at a time, increasing as the lips strengthen.

To make a start, fold the lower lip over the teeth to make a cushion on which the blade of the reed rests, and then bring the upper lip down on to the top of the reed. About half of the reed blade should be in the mouth and the amount of tension, or grip, must be determined by experiment. The best instruction which can be given in writing is to pinch the reed very slightly with your lips, increasing until success crowns your efforts with a sound. At the same time place the tip of the tongue against the tip of the reed and, having taken a deep breath, articulate the sound TA (as in TAP) while expelling the breath.

At this stage every note should be started with this rather explosive TA, to avoid any resemblance to the old fashioned bleating sound, when bassoons felt their way in (often late) with no precise start to the note. With progress the explosive attack must be diminished, always having regard, however, for the definite start to every note, in the right place, which good playing demands.

This action will cause the blades of the reed to vibrate.

reath and play a long, even note *mf*, and be
at there is no variation in pitch nor in quality of
ther of these defects would be caused by jerky
or uneven lip pressure. Eight or ten long notes
done at each practice, and when a good steady
tained without difficulty gradations of tone should
luced as follows; first on C and then on all the
es.

ow time to find some more notes on the instrument.
fingering chart find the two lowest notes on the

B♮ and B♭, 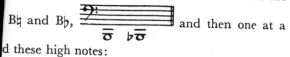 and then one at a

d these high notes:

he time being this should be regarded as the effective
f the bassoon—three octaves. Some higher notes can
d later.

ng arrived at this point let us examine some of the

At first you may find it difficult to produce any sound at
all. So check the following points:

(a) Is the reed gripped too tightly?—or too loosely?
(b) Are you breathing out evenly?
(c) Is the reed too far in your mouth?

A little experiment should result in a sound. Possibly an
odd sound, but still a sound.

A steady flow of air is essential for a good sound, and
without it the tone is weak and strangled.

Following these instructions, and fingering the note C
as shown above, try again. This time start to breathe out a
little *before* saying TA. Repeat this several times. Now lift
the third finger* of the left hand. This will give D,
. Lifting the second finger as well will give E,
and lifting up the first finger too (all three fingers off) will
give F. Try each of these notes many times.

The bassoon must be supported by the lower part of the
first finger. These left-hand fingers should be arched and
when lifted should not be raised very far from the holes, for
obvious reasons.

Now for the right hand, first having replaced the three
fingers of the left hand on to the holes. Cover the top hole
of the double joint with the first finger of the right hand.
This will give you B, . The addition of the
second finger on the next hole will give A. The third
finger is then placed on the second silver key to give G,
and the fourth finger (little finger) presses down the higher
of the two remaining keys to give low F.

It may be, at first, that some, or all, of these notes fail to
come. This may be caused by the fingers not quite covering
some of the holes. Check particularly the third finger of
left hand as the stretch between second and third fingers
is a wide one, and the third finger tends to pull upwards

* For bassoon playing we use the terms thumb, first, second, third,
and fourth fingers.

and off the hole. Check also that some other key on the instrument is not being inadvertently moved.

Play up and down this scale with varying lengths of notes, and speeds, until you feel at home with it.

To increase the 'repertoire' add G to the top of the scale . The fingering for this note is the same as the G an octave below, but with the top hole (F) only *half* closed by the first finger of left hand. To obtain this 'half-hole' the first finger should be 'rolled' over, and *not* lifted and replaced in the new position.

Now find on your fingering chart the notes

and

You can now play a two-octave major scale from C to C,

. From the fingering chart find the extra notes in this order:—B♭ (*always* using the back thumb key with the right hand), F♯, E♭, C♯, G♯. And now you can play a *chromatic* scale in two octaves. The octave key should be closed for all notes below F , and of course open for all notes above it. F itself is optional, depending on the instrument.

On the tenor joint there are three keys for the left hand thumb. The lowest one is the key which produces C♯, and the other two keys are called 'speaker keys'. They must be used whenever possible for the notes A, B♭, B♮, and C, . The lower of the two keys is used for A, and the higher one for B♭, B♮, and C. These 'speaker keys' make the notes doubly safe and cause them to respond quickly. Some British players do not use them, but I myself think they are essential. On many bassoons

---

F to B♭ played legato is 'st[

speaker key makes this com[many hazardous descents a[shown later. There is a thir[bassoons (see Chapter X).

You will now be playing [only as separate notes, eac[slurring several together, th[change from note to note wi[of the finger movements a[like this:

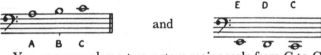

1.

2.

3.

4.

(* For F to G see later in this chap[

Every day some 'long note' [this is an essential part of every[from the beginner to the exper[

at first a good solid note—for ir[

a deep [careful t[tone. Ei[breathin[should b[tone is o[be intro[other no[

It is [On you[

bassoon[

time fir[

For [range [be add[Hav[

difficulties which may have arisen on the way. An early troublesome hazard is how to make a smooth change from

F to G . All fingers *off* to five and a half

fingers *on!* Unless they all arrive *on* exactly together the result is disastrous. The fingers must move very rapidly, with an accent in each finger, and almost a 'snatch' at first. This applies to all similar difficulties where several fingers have to move.

Low E to F♯ can be tricky also, . The

thumb on the E key should *almost* touch the F♯ key when the E is being played, and should then slide and roll on to the F♯ key instead of making a jump for it.

Another point; you may have found that blowing every note in exactly the same way results in some notes being out of tune. Most probably the higher notes will be flat. The ear must take special care here, and a slight adjustment of lip pressure must be made to bring all the notes in line. Intonation is dealt with more fully in a later chapter, but a general rule for this early difficulty is to tighten the lips a little as you go up the scale, and slacken them slightly as you come down.

I cannot stress too strongly the importance of relaxation throughout the practice and playing of the bassoon; and each page of this book should really bear the heading 'relax' in large type. A certain tension inevitably creeps in with the beginner who is striving with unfamiliar tools and pulling unfamilar faces. But this causes unnecessary tiredness and strain. You must be alert to the necessity for constant relaxation, and endeavour to look and feel as though you were enjoying it, as indeed you are, and be strengthened by the thought that in due course other people will enjoy your efforts too.

BREATH CONTROL AND TONE

Breath control plays a large part in the successful playing of all wind instruments. Most people use only a portion of their lungs. To obtain a steady, even, and regular flow of air into the instrument it is necessary to use the whole of the lungs, and to do this naturally requires considerable thought and training.

It is not too much to say that everyone would benefit in health by following the rules of breathing which every wind player has to observe. I know of many authenticated cases where persistent respiratory troubles were cured by the sufferers taking up a woodwind instrument and learning to breathe properly.

Stand upright and take a deep breath. I think you will find that only the top part of your lungs is inflated. Try to force the air downwards as far as you can. Check on this by placing your hands against your sides, below the ribs. If a definite 'bellows' movement can be felt all is going well. If not try again and again, and soon this deep breathing should become natural. It should almost feel as though you were breathing from your stomach, but what is happening, of course, is that the diaphragm and the lower part of the lungs are being used. Practise inhaling slowly and deeply, and exhaling slowly and evenly. It is important that this should be done without raising the shoulders at all and without any stiffness anywhere. When this can be done comfortably, practise *in*haling more quickly (and through the mouth) and *ex*haling as slowly as possible, again keeping the outward flow of air as even as you can. This is how you breathe when playing the bassoon, and the exercise can be done at any time, at first away from the instrument.

With this kind of deep breathing long melodic passages can be played without the disfigurement caused by a number of breath gaps. Solo passages similar to this well-known one from Tchaikovsky's Fourth Symphony can be played with ease, and with only one breath gap where indicated—to the great gain of the music:

Variation in dynamics and pitch on the bassoon are produced by the speed and volume of the airstream directed into the instrument through the reed.

Breathing should never be obvious. It should be the slave and not the master of the music, and should provide the punctuation in musical phrases in the same way as it does in speech.

Tone

Breath control is vital to the production of a good tone. Although quality of tone is determined to a certain extent by the reed (and, of course, the instrument) that is by no means the whole picture. Tone is something essentially personal to the player, something which can never be taught and rarely explained. No two players will produce the same tone on the same instrument, and a good tone is the mark of the fine musician. Ultimately a player will have the tone that his ear demands.

I have in mind a clever scientist (an amateur musician) who, by means of the most delicate scientific instruments, measured the pressures, stresses, air-speeds, etc., etc., inside the mouths and instruments of several famous players, on the same instrument and reed. From his calculations he reasoned that if he could reproduce exactly the same conditions when he played the instrument, he would have a similar tone quality. Alas for science! The experiment failed, for the fine player's artistic ear and sensitivity is responsible for the tone and this cannot be measured.

However, at this stage we are concerned more with the student who, rather at the mercy of his instrument and reed, sometimes imagines that a good tone is beyond him, until (a) he possesses the finest of all instruments, and a perfect reed; or (b) he has so mastered his technique that he can at last tackle this matter of improving the sound he is producing. This is not the right approach. Once the initial scale of notes has been mastered, and the lips have become accustomed to the reed, you should set about trying to produce the tone you are really aiming to possess. From the very beginning, on long notes and in simple melodies, try to achieve this, and also try to persuade your instrument to co-operate. Never be satisfied with less.

Listen to the finest bassoon-players; listen to the finest players on all woodwind instruments. More than this, listen to the greatest players on string instruments and to the best singers. You have something to learn from them all. I myself derived the greatest possible help from listening to Kreisler and Casals.

FINGER TECHNIQUE

The basis on which an adequate finger technique is built is the regular practice of scales and arpeggios. This is the only way to produce fluent and even passage playing, and it is also a tremendous help in reading.

A passage like this for instance is not read note by note, but is immediately recognized as the dominant seventh of B major:

At the end of this chapter I have written out two scales, one major and the other minor, as a pattern to work from. There are many forms possible and this is the one I recommend.

Whole tone scales are particularly useful as a preparation for much modern music, and chromatic scales also must be practised.

All the scales should be gone through, starting with C major and A minor; then F major and D minor; then G major and E minor; and so on through the whole range. All from memory. Some pupils, from time to time, have told me that they could not play the scales without the music. This is really a form of laziness. Certainly a scale book is useful, but it is far more valuable to be able to play them from memory at any moment; and you will later realize what confidence this gives.

I suggest that one scale, and one scale only, should be

worked at until the finished product is as perfect as can be contrived. Then go on to the next scale.

Many people incline to the belief that scale practice is dull, but if worked at properly it can be fascinating. To the thrill of overcoming difficulties can be added the satisfaction in the steady, and often rapid, improvement in finger technique and control. But you must remember to relax all the time, and to guard against lifting the fingers too high, for this is a waste of time and leads to inaccuracy.

From scales to studies. Studies must always occupy a large part of the practising time. I recommend Weissenborn Op. 8, Books 1 and 2, followed by Milde *Scale and Chord Studies* and his *Concert Studies*, Books 1 and 2. These books will keep you occupied for years, as, unlike many study books, which are often rather dull, these are of musical interest as well. Practise slowly and increase speed gradually.

I want to stress here the vital necessity of learning how to practise properly. There are many most earnest and conscientious students who blithely recount the hours they have spent at work each day, cheerfully believing that their progress will match the hands of the clock, speeding onwards. To listen to them practising is often to be very disappointed. Most of the time is virtually wasted effort. They will play through scales and studies many times, making the same mistakes each time. If they are aware of them and go back, they will play the whole thing again, instead of picking out the naughty bits and working at them with great concentration until they are correct. Other times they will pick out the bits they like to play and do these over and over again, while the tricky passage lurks round the corner and trips them up almost unnoticed! Ten minutes hard work at a few little bits is worth hours of aimless 'playing'.

Pick out the parts you cannot play and work at them. Break up a difficult passage into small pieces and work at each one. Then join them up. Here is an example. Not very difficult, but a little tricky:

First play the section marked A time after time, slowly, until it is safe. Then practise section B. Join A and B together at varying speeds.

Follow this with section C and then join B and C. Practise section D and join this to C. Then play the whole passage slowly, gradually getting it quicker. In a short time this will be fluent and cause no more trouble, and this pattern should be followed for all passage practice; it is a good idea to invent little exercises on these lines, to cope with any special difficulties.

I have sometimes been told by a new pupil that he has 'done' certain study books. When I have pointed out a particularly good study and enquired how he got on with it the reply would be, 'Oh, I haven't done that one. I didn't particularly like it'. It then turns out that only about half the studies in the book had been 'done', and those very inadequately. It is a mistake to jump about picking studies here and there in a book. They are carefully graded, each one dealing with a special point, and should be practised in the right order.

SELECTED SCALES AND ARPEGGIOS

C major

Dom. 7th

and so on.

and so on.

A minor

1.

2.

Dim. 7th

3.

4.

5.

6.

and so on

7.

8.

Chromatic Scale

Whole-tone Scales

Every exercise should be practised in each of the following ways and in all keys major and minor.

If you cannot play the high notes at first go as high as you can and then turn back.

INTONATION

The notes on a bassoon are more capricious than on any other woodwind instrument. This is partly due to the size and shape of the instrument, and to the fact that some of the holes have to be bored at an angle to enable the fingers to cover them. Therefore more care must be taken with intonation on the bassoon than on other woodwind instruments. Good ear training is essential so that the necessary adjustments can be made.

As I said in an earlier chapter, the top register will tend to be a little flat if the same lip pressures and blowing are used for the high notes as are used for the lower ones. Consequently an adjustment of pressure must be made all the time—a tighter lip pressure as you go up the instrument, and a slacker pressure as you go down. Care must be taken not to overdo these changes of lip pressure, and the only guide to this is, of course, the ear.

In addition, all bassoons have some notes which respond differently, and need slightly different airspeeds and pressures (middle G is sharp on many instruments) and these adjustments will soon become automatic if the ear is sufficiently alert.

Care must also be taken when the volume of sound is increased, for with the greater air pressure forced through the reed the sound frequently sharpens, so a compensatory slackening, probably very slight, must be made by the lips. This is another reason why 'long-note' practice is so valuable.

Because of these little problems of intonation the bassoon is really the most *personal* of all instruments, each instrument differing from every other one. This is part of its charm, no doubt, but it will be readily understood why no bassoon player can pick up someone else's instrument and play on it with a good intonation right away. It may take months to become at home on a different one. Exercises for intonation can be devised, and arpeggio practice—done slowly—is very helpful if you listen carefully to every note.

This is a good exercise. The higher octave note must be clearly *heard* in your head, before it is played.

And here is another one:

You can invent similar exercises on these patterns.

When you play in an orchestra, or with other people, and there is some faulty intonation around, do, *please*, be the shining example and assume it is probably you who are out of tune—and act accordingly—instead of waiting complacently for the others to put matters right!

When there is some discrepancy of intonation in an orchestra, there are times when the offender finds it difficult to know whether he is slightly flat or sharp. This may be when the clash occurs between instruments playing at wide range (for example, bassoon and piccolo). At these times you must try to push it the way you feel most likely, but be ready to adjust the other way if it does not correct the trouble. In an orchestra you must remember there are problems of intonation which you will not meet elsewhere. Violins, for instance, frequently go sharp as they play higher notes (one of the minor mysteries), and cellos and basses are often sharp on their lowest strings. For the sake of the performance one has to humour them, and accompany them at least part of the way.

I am going to say a few words now to the more advanced student. It happens occasionally that one of you will come along in some distress, and complain that you feel you are playing consistently sharp nowadays, and have even been told so by your colleagues, and perhaps by a conductor. This is the reason. Over recent years your embouchure has strengthened and altered a little—so gradually that you have not realized it—with the result that the pressures you used in your earlier days are now, in conjunction with your stronger lip, too fierce. If you have been chided for this in an orchestra you may, in your anxiety, have made matters even worse by tightening still more. To deal with this, *relax*, and take a little less reed in the mouth—and then relax all over again.

VI

STACCATO

A good reliable staccato is one of the brightest jewels in the bassoon player's crown! To achieve this requires careful thought and, of course, much practice.

The position of the tongue in relation to the tip of the reed is most important. The usual instruction, years ago, was to 'hit the tip of the reed with the tip of the tongue'. When I was a young student I could make no headway with this, so, experimenting for myself, I found my staccato greatly improved when I rolled the tip of my tongue downward slightly, touching the reed about $\frac{1}{8}''$ or $\frac{1}{4}''$ *above* the tip of the tongue. This, I think, is the normal position for most players, but tooth structure and the shape of the mouth may require modifications and you must experiment for yourself. The important thing is that the position decided on should allow a comfortable movement of the tongue without any stiffening.

Having placed the tongue against the tip of the reed, articulate a very short TA. This will result in the tongue returning to the reed tip quickly. The quality of the staccato note produced is determined by the speed with which the breath enters the reed, and the length of the note is decided by the time taken by the tongue to return to its position against the reed.

Try this:  over

and over again, playing the notes as short as possible, and with plenty of tongue movement, as this will help to prevent any stiffening of the tongue and throat muscles, which is fatal to staccato. When the tongue is working fairly well at a slow speed try it a little quicker. At the first sign of any stiffness or tiredness practice should be abandoned for a few minutes.

This is a good exercise:

It should always be played with a good rhythm, on different notes, and the rhythmic changes clearly defined.

Another exercise:

and so on.
Then down again.

Very often a lack of synchronization occurs here between fingers and tongue; it is usually the fingers that are at fault, as the player's attention is centred on the tongue.

This passage:  might sound rather like this: . To overcome this

difficulty play the passage slowly, lifting the appropriate fingers smartly, and lowering them smartly (and with a slight accent) for the corresponding falling passage. A gradual increase of speed and careful practice should solve this problem.

The tongue should always move rapidly, so that in staccato at slow speeds there will be a period when it does not move at all, but rests against the reed. As the pace increases the gap will become shorter.

Practise longer passages and increase the pace gradually:

and so on.

Never try a rapid pace until the slow speeds are under control. Think of a small rubber ball bouncing along.

I have met many players who could 'tongue' rapidly, and also slowly, but were defeated by the intermediate speeds. This is a most worrying state of affairs, so make sure you practise *all* speeds.

Various rhythms must be tried as follows:

In your practice of staccato, I repeat, make all notes as short as possible. It is a simple matter to lengthen them if required.

Double-tonguing is used by a few players, but it is not really entirely satisfactory, and I never use it myself. The end product is not so clean and even as single tonguing. Instead of the single syllable 'TA', the player goes 'TA-KA' or 'TOO-KOO'. It cannot be used at slow speed and where a change has to be made from quick staccato to slow (i.e. from double to single), or where there is a gradual ritardando, the change of gear is almost always very apparent. Also, a player who has cultivated double-tonguing rarely has a good single tongue staccato.

(*)Some players on all instruments find this last rhythmic passage tricky. Try saying the word 'Amsterdam' over and over again, as that gives the exact rhythm. It is a rhythm which occurs frequently in the first movement of Beethoven's Seventh Symphony.

I would suggest that a good single tongue staccato **can** meet all requirements, and it should be worked at until **it** can sign itself 'your obedient servant'.

VIBRATO, RUBATO, AND BAD HABITS

There are various opinions regarding the use of vibrato. It seems to be generally agreed that a small amount of vibrato can give life, warmth, and vitality to the tone. I suggest that 'small' should be the operative word.

The wide, throbbing type of vibrato—wow-wow, wow-wow—is in bad taste, in my opinion, whether it is vocal or instrumental, and can easily make a bassoon sound like a badly played saxophone. I have heard this sort of sound described rather aptly as resembling 'a jelly at bay'!

There is certainly one advantage possessed by the perpetrator of this kind of vibrato; if his wobble is sufficiently wide he can reckon on being in tune for part of the time! In some cases it is used to disguise a poor tone, or inferior finger technique, but it does not accomplish this very successfully.

I suggest that vibrato should be used on the bassoon with great care. Certain passages in more recent work could gain by its use, but there is a great deal to be said for a clean, pure tone, particularly in the classics. There are various ways of producing this 'problem child': by the diaphragm, the throat, or the lip.

A famous woodwind player was asked by a pupil to explain how the attractive, small vibrato, which he occasionally used in certain solo passages, was done. He looked at the pupil with great surprise and said: 'That can't be *taught*. If the music calls for it you do it, if not, you don't. Generally you don't!'

Its indiscriminate use in the woodwind department of an orchestra can be very disturbing, for it distorts the harmonic structure. In this connection, I have heard many performances of the Beethoven Choral Symphony where the vocal quartet in the Finale has been ruined by the excessive vibrato of the singers. In one performance I have in mind all four singers had such wide and wobbly vibratos that not a single chord could be identified.

I asked the principal bassoonist of a famous continental orchestra his views on this subject. His answer was: 'Any player who uses vibrato in the classics should be shot'. Drastic, but effective!

Rubato

Rubato, which is robbing the time at one place to pay it back later, must be used with great discretion, and only by the mature and thoroughly musical player on rare occasions. Otherwise it becomes bad taste. It can be used to point an essential note in a melodic phrase. Here is an example:

It is for two bassoons and is from the second movement of Mozart's 'Jupiter' Symphony. An almost imperceptible tenuto on the high note illuminates the phrase. Too much would sound vulgar and would also upset the string accompaniment.

I remember the conductor Hans Richter addressing a wind player, who was rather given to overdoing it: 'Sir, Rubato, a little, then and now, yes! But always, My God, never!'

Bad habits

Beating Time with the Foot is a bad habit. It is annoying to other players, and is almost useless if the desired end is to play in strict time. The foot follows the player's inclinations, and if the playing slows down so does the foot. If you feel you are a little shaky on rhythm it would be helpful if you could get a friend to check it for you by tapping your shoulder in strict time as you play; provided, of course, the friend's rhythm is impeccable and not the same as yours! A metronome can sometimes serve a useful purpose if used occasionally as a check.

If a pupil has a poor sense of rhythm I tell him to *imagine* a large pendulum swinging to and fro across the wall, and to play with it.

Slovenly attitudes

I occasionally come across people who think it is rather clever to give an impression of casual nonchalance when playing. They sit or stand in a careless attitude and affect to be uninterested in what is going on. Slovenly attitudes or careless behaviour produce slovenly and careless playing.

Playing after the beat

When you are playing with others—in chamber music, or orchestra—guard against being a little after the beat. Remember the instrument takes a fraction of time to 'speak'; if this is not watched and allowed for, you can develop a habit of being always a little late. This is irritating and will make you very unpopular.

Mannerisms

It is inevitable that, as players develop their musical personalities, certain little mannerisms will creep in when they are playing.

You should always be on the watch to see that these never become excessive. For instance, swaying about when playing in an orchestra can be most annoying to one's neighbours. Grunts and groans, excessive fidgeting with reed and instrument, and pulling unnecessary faces, will also not endear you to your colleagues.

In addition, never allow yourself to puff your cheeks out when blowing.

Blowing moisture out

Never blow moisture out of the holes or crook, nor blow through the reed in a noisy manner in public. It is, of course, extremely important to ensure that the holes are kept free of moisture. If this is neglected an odd drop of moisture may find its way into one or more of the holes as a result of condensation, which can be quite disastrous, causing those notes to fail, or producing extraordinary noises. Experienced players take every precaution against this by blowing down the holes from time to time; but don't get into a habit of making a great deal of fuss and noise about it, and being a nuisance on a platform.

VIII

TENOR CLEF

The tenor clef is freely used in bassoon music (as in cello music) and if approached intelligently it will present no difficulty. Don't make the mistake of reading the notes as if they were bass (or treble) and then making the necessary calculations. In other words don't do it by transposing all the time. Learn the lines and spaces of the stave in tenor clef so that the notes are recognized at once. In bass clef middle C is here: 𝄢 but in tenor clef it comes here: 𝄡. This can be learned very quickly, and also the few notes round about it. It will be seen that the great advantage of tenor clef is that it avoids the use of many leger lines when the music goes above middle C. It is only a matter of practice to get completely familiar with the higher and lower notes in tenor clef.

Certain composers make use of the lower leger lines rather freely. Bizet and Auber for example. Here is an example for bassoons from Bizet's *L'Arlésienne* Suite. The second bassoon here goes down to low F:

ALLEGRO DECISO *Tempo di marcia*

IX

REEDS

Before dealing with the reed itself I want to make some remarks about the whole problem.

Whereas it is essential to realize the importance of the reed on tone, intonation, and even on the production of the actual notes, it is very easy to over-emphasize the part it should play in your life. One constantly meets people who are obsessed by reeds. They cannot play a solo; they dare not try such-and-such a passage—they haven't a good enough reed! Still worse are those who make it the scapegoat for faulty playing, poor tone, missing the notes, etc.—they had such a poor reed!

It is a vicious circle, as their confidence and even ability comes to depend on this little bit of cane; they have sleepless nights before concerts, spend their waking hours fiddling with tools and cane, and, having discarded most of their reeds, end up no doubt on the psychiatrist's couch. This is a deplorable state of affairs and should never be allowed.

There is a sharp lesson to be learned from this story. Some years ago, a young boy I happen to know rather well was playing quite a difficult solo at school. The tone was good, and the performance really very pleasant. Afterwards I said: 'Let me look at your reed.' I was astonished to find that not only was one side stuck with sellotape, but that a large piece at the corner was broken right off. Anyone who knew anything about reeds would know that it 'couldn't play'! I was surprised that any sound came out at all. When I remarked that it didn't look very good the reply was: 'Oh, that! I've been using it for months, I can't fuss about a reed!' Out of the mouths . . .!

You must learn to play on a *fair* reed, and if a good one comes along regard it as an Act of God.

Having agreed on this point, let us turn our attention to seeing what can be done to get as good a reed as possible. It is essential that from the beginning you should know how to adapt the reeds you buy to suit yourself and the instrument. This is important, and what most people do all their lives. Later on, you should learn how to make a reed from the beginning, and I have put some notes on this at the end of this chapter. But I do not advise you to make your own as a general rule because too much valuable practising time can be swallowed up by this lengthy and exacting occupation. Most players buy their reeds from special reed makers. If you buy them ready for use, you may find that only a small proportion of them will suit you. This is because what is good for one player may not suit another, and it is wiser to buy 'hard', or 'unfinished' reeds (as I do), and perform the finishing stage yourself.

It is advisable to decide as early as possible what type of reed is best for your use. You will aim for one that gives a good quality of tone; that is easy to blow both on high and low notes; that 'speaks' quickly, and gives a good intonation all over the instrument. We have already decided that it is rare to find such a reed, but a great deal can be done quite simply to one of these 'unfinished' reeds, once you have acquired a little knowledge and aptitude. You will need these tools: a sharp knife; a small pair of pliers; soft brass wire; two files, coarse and fine (if possible knife-edged); a mandril; a 'reed-tongue'; fine sandpaper, or better still Dutch rush or shave-grass. You can get this equipment from some instrument makers.

The blade of a reed should taper gradually from the wire to the tip; and from the middle of the reed to the sides. In this diagram the shaded portion is called the 'heart' of the reed, and should only be touched as a last resort. Take your 'hard' or 'unfinished' reed and place it in cold water for a few minutes. Insert the reed-tongue between the blades of cane. The reed must be held in such a way that

Diagram No. 1.

the thick part of the first finger of the left hand must—repeat, must—be placed underneath the tip of the blades before any scraping is attempted. Otherwise the lower blade will split as soon as any pressure is put on the top blade. This is important.

Then, with your knife, scrape gently away from the middle to the corners; that is, the *un*shaded part in the diagram, removing only a very small amount of cane. Try the reed on the bassoon, blowing a few notes. If it still does not 'speak' as it should, repeat the operation until it does, finishing off by applying a piece of sand-paper or Dutch rush. It is better to leave the reed a little on the hard side, as it should mellow with use. This is the basic treatment, but here are a few hints for improving the reed.

If the reed sounds dull and lifeless, thin the extreme tip slightly. If the low notes are hard to produce, thin the tip, going a little further back towards the wire. If a reed sounds brittle and harsh, thin the sides from the tip right down to the wire. A reed can be made a little more free by scraping both blades near the wire. Sometimes a reed is improved by a gentle rubbing all over with fine sand-paper.

At all times only a very little is removed.

A reed that is flat in pitch, or too soft to blow, should have a very thin slice cut off the tips of the blades.

An old, worn out reed can sometimes be revived in this way.

Occasionally a reed may leak near the wires, owing to some carelessness in the making, and here a little colourless nail-varnish may be applied. If the blades are too close together the reed will not vibrate properly. To remedy this, apply your pliers to the wire nearest the blades, very gently, at the sides, which will open the blades. This may make the reed a little harder. Pliers applied to the *second* wire, not this time at the sides, but at the top and bottom (closing the throat), will also open the blades, and this is not so likely to make the reed harder.

It is essential to preserve the 'heart' of the reed. Any undue thinning here will result in poor tone, bad intonation, and general uncertainty.

There are other little adjustments which can be made, but only experience will teach these.

Cleaning reeds

After a certain amount of use a reed becomes clogged inside, and is therefore less responsive, and is hard to play. The deposit must be removed, and it is customary to clean it out with a feather or needle. This often results in the reed becoming thin and nasal in sound, due to the fibres inside being disturbed. I prefer to soak the reed first of all for about an hour, and then to force the deposit out with water. I use an antisplash rubber nozzle which fits over the cold tap, and, placing the base of the reed against this nozzle, I turn the tap full on.

Making a reed

Whole pieces of cane can be bought but usually one buys it split, and cut to a convenient length. This will be ready gouged, and should be rather thicker in the middle and tapering towards the sides. The piece of cane is soaked in cold water for about two hours. This is to prevent it splitting. Then small nicks are made at each side, dead centre of the cane, as in Diagram No. 2. The bark is cut off for about $1\frac{1}{2}''$ above and below the centre (that is, the shaded portion on the diagram), leaving the cane thinner and thinner as the centre is approached.

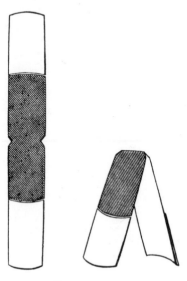

Diagrams 2 and 3.

Now look at Diagram No. 3. The cane is doubled back, over a knife blade, taking care to squeeze the thin portion quickly against the knife blade, so that it does not gape, and render succeeding operations more difficult.

Most makers use a 'shape' for the next operation. The cane is fastened to the 'shape' and the sides pared off with a sharp knife. I prefer to shape my reeds myself, as follows. In pencil, mark off the position of the three wires B, C and D; also the outline of the required shape (see Diagram No. 4). Take your measurements from a good reed of your own. With a sharp knife cut away the unwanted cane, leaving a small margin outside the pencilled lines. With the file take away the margin from A to B (on each side), leaving A to B perfectly straight. This is important to prevent later leakage. The width of the throat at BB should be the same as at CC. It should widen slightly from CC to DD. Finish off B to D (both sides) with a knife, and smooth with a file. Now you can see some slight resemblance to the finished reed (Diagram No. 5).

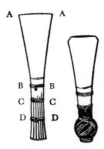

Diagrams 4 and 5.

Wrap the whole reed, from $\frac{1}{4}''$ below A to within $\frac{1}{4}''$ of the bottom of the cane, with cord or string, keeping it fairly tight all the way, but *much* tighter towards B.

From the bottom of the cane, to where the wrapping begins, diagonal cuts are made through the cane with a sharp knife and the greased mandril is carefully inserted. This is assisted by finger manipulation and later by gentle pressure with the pliers from B to D. The base of the reed should now have been coaxed into a perfectly round aperture. Measure the depth of your good reed's base and mark the mandril to guide you as to how far the mandril should be inserted. Remove the cord wrapping from the base and put on the wires in this order: D, C and B. Wire D will, of course, be elliptical, and until recently wire C was always made round. Nowadays some leading makers favour an *oval* wire C.

D

Next, cut all bark away from the blades (having removed rest of wrapping) down to $\frac{1}{8}''$ above wire B. Thin the blades considerably now, bearing in mind that we want a gradual taper from base to tip, and from middle to sides. Cut off the tip with a sharp razor or knife and trim the base of the reed.

If the reed has been accurately made, the base should be quite round and should fit on the crook with no airleak. If it is not quite round a rat-tailed file must be obtained and gently used inside. Wrap the base of the reed from C to the end with macrame cord, copying the method from your own reed, and coat it with shellac.

At this stage leave the reed to settle for some days and then finish off according to the instructions in the first part of this chapter.

FURTHER HINTS AND ADVICE

Some technical hints

In Chapter II, I mentioned the 'speaker-keys', and how certain legato moves downward are rendered safer and smoother by their use. In the following examples the higher speaker-key is used for B and B♭ in the first two, and the lower speaker-key for the A in the third example:

On some modern bassoons there are three speaker-keys. The extra one is added above the other two, and is used *only* to facilitate the extreme high notes. These are C♯, D and E♭.

This extra speaker-key is shown in plate I.

On some bassoons the following legato progressions are uncertain:

For the E♭ and E♮ in these examples, lift the first finger of the right hand to make them speak more freely. An alternative suggestion is to add the C♯ key (thumb of the left hand) to the normal fingerings, leaving the C♯ key as soon as the notes 'speak'.

To improve notes which are doubtful on some instruments, I suggest the following:

1.

Add low D key (thumb of left hand) to normal fingering.

2.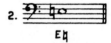

Sometimes flat with a soft reed. Add low E key (thumb of right hand).

3.

Frequently an unstable note, so add low C♯ key (little finger of left hand), or low D key, as above.

4.

For a better and fuller note, add three fingers of right hand and fourth finger on F key. If this is too flat, lift first finger of right hand.

5.

For a full, safe note, add second and third fingers of right hand with fourth finger on the F key.

6.

For a fuller note, add low E♭ key (fourth finger of left hand).

7.

Bb   B♮   C

If flat, these three notes can be made sharper by adding the B♭ key (thumb of right hand).

Some musical hints

When the notes rise in the music, let the tone increase. Of course there are exceptions to this but it is a good general rule to follow. As the bassoon plays a considerable amount of accompanying passages and counter-melodies in orchestral music, care must be taken to see that the tone quality and, indeed, the general style of playing, is never allowed to become dull or uninteresting. In this connection, exaggerate the marks of expression.

In a passage comprising slurred and staccato notes give the first legato note a slight accent.

Trills should always be practised slowly and evenly at first. Always decide exactly how many notes are to be played in the trill, and do not let your fingers flap up and down aimlessly.

In technical passages with complicated fingering, do not be tempted to use alternative fake fingerings for certain notes. They only lead to disaster. They may sound very well at home, when recommended by a well-meaning friend, but in the stress of the moment at a concert it may well be quite another matter.

Tuning

When an instrument is cold it will play very flat. Consequently you must always give yourself a few minutes to warm it up by playing on it, before you settle down to play seriously. The difference in pitch between a cold and a warm instrument is very great. Have the correct tuning fork (A = 440) and check with it frequently.

Most of the difficult passages which you will meet in orchestral music, except in extremely modern works, are based on the scales and arpeggios that you have studied.

To finish this chapter I append a few difficult passages for bassoon, taken from well-known orchestral works which you may meet, and give you a few hints regarding their treatment.

EXCERPT No. 1. The opening of Mozart's 'Marriage of Figaro' Overture

This is most difficult to play smoothly and evenly at speed, particularly as it must be played very quietly. When the passage returns in the middle of the Overture it is even more difficult. Practise this very slowly, *always* softly, and with a slight accent on the first note of each phrase. Gradually quicken and omit the accent, until satisfactorily up to speed.

EXCERPT No. 2. Finale of Beethoven's Fourth Symphony

The famous solo staccato passage in the last movement is always one of the tests you will be asked to play at an audition. Although it is marked 'Allegro ma non troppo', some conductors take it 'Presto' which makes it very hazardous. The start of this passage is generally inaudible, owing to other orchestral sounds, and I therefore suggest that the first two notes should be played *slurred* which makes for a firmer start with more tone. If the tempo is abnormally quick, the two notes at the *top* of the passage can also be slurred with advantage to the general shape and rhythm.

EXCERPT No. 3. Last Movement of Borodin's Second Symphony

This two bar passage requires very rapid finger change. It should be practised very slowly and makes an excellent study in itself.

EXCERPT No. 4. Waltz Movement from Tchaikovsky's Fifth Symphony

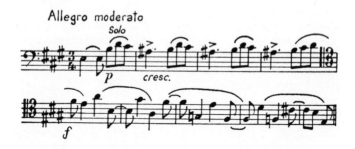

This is a good example of the need for 'speaker-keys'. The slurs from high A down to B, and from high G♯ to A, would be found extremely difficult without their use. Be very careful of the half-hole opening in high G♯.

EXCERPT No. 5. First Movement of Tchaikovsky's 'Pathétique' Symphony (No. 6)

A special soft reed should be used for the very important opening of this movement. Take great care to observe the dynamics, and remember that when playing softly on the low notes, all finger holes and keys should be closed very firmly.

EXCERPT No. 6. Another example from the same Movement as No. 5

This consists of only four notes, but it is marked *pppppp!!* It follows, and indeed terminates, the clarinet cadenza, and is usually played on the bass clarinet as it is much easier to play low notes softly on this instrument. When there is no bass clarinet available it is played on the bassoon. Some players advocate stuffing a handkerchief down the bell to mute the sound, but I do not advise this as it spoils the tone. A special *very* soft reed would help. These last two examples are the only occasions when I would agree that a reed should be changed during a performance.

EXCERPT No. 7. Second Movement of Rimsky-Korsakov's 'Scheherazade'

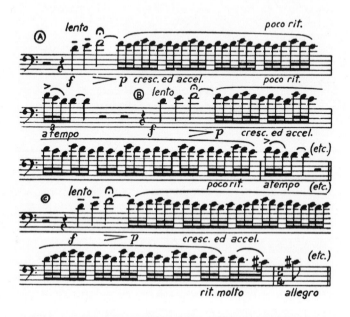

These three cadenza passages, each more difficult than the last, make an excellent finger study. This is the classic example of when *not* to use fake fingerings, in spite of any advice to the contrary. Needless to say they must be practised very slowly, but when playing them at a performance start each one rather slowly, quickening appreciably in the middle, and slowing off towards the last few notes, which of course are 'in tempo'. To avoid monotony let the beginning of each one start a *little* slower than the previous one. Never try to play it so fast that the notes are not clear.

EXCERPT No. 8. Stravinsky's 'Rite of Spring'

This extraordinary solo passage, which opens the work, created consternation amongst bassoon players when it first appeared. It is reported that, when questioned about it, Stravinsky said he wished it to sound 'as if striving for the unattainable'. That is all very well, but it must be played, and nowadays, with our improved techniques, it is played as a matter of course. There is no magic formula. The notes are there and once again familiarity will breed, if not contempt, at least some degree of comfort, so it is a passage to be practised frequently, and carefully worked out. It is a great help in reaching the top D if you 'hear' the note in your head first. This, of course, applies to all high notes.

When you can play all these passages (and others like them) confidently, easily, correctly and musically, you can pass this book over to a friend.

APPENDIX

A LIST OF MUSIC FOR THE BASSOON

Compiled by William Waterhouse

The following list aims to be fairly exhaustive only with regard to solo music for bassoon. In view of the vast amount of chamber music which calls for the bassoon, a selection has been made of the most important and useful works from the repertoire which, it is hoped, will be of more practical use than an exhaustive list. For a complete catalogue of chamber music, the following two reference works should be consulted:

Kammermusik Katalog (music printed 1841-1944) by Wilhelm Altmann, Hofmeister, Leipzig. 1945.

Kammermusik Katalog (music printed 1944-58) by Johannes F. Richter, Hofmeister, Leipzig. 1960.

The list is arranged as follows:

Bassoon and orchestra
Solo instruments and orchestra
Bassoon and piano
Bassoons only
Chamber music for bassoon and strings
Miscellaneous chamber music

ABBREVIATIONS

fl	flute	trp	trumpet	trio	oboe, clarinet,
ob	oboe	trb	trombone		bassoon
cor ang	cor anglais	vn	violin	str qt	string quartet
cl	clarinet	va	viola	quintet	flute, oboe,
basset hn	basset horn	vc	cello		clarinet, horn,
					bassoon
bcl	bass clarinet	cb	bass		
bn	bassoon	hp	harp		
cbn	contra bassoon				
hn	horn	pf	piano		
sax	saxophone	cont	continuo		

A SHORT SELECTED LIST OF AGENTS IN GREAT BRITAIN FOR MUSIC PUBLISHED ABROAD

BELGIUM: Hinrichsen, 10-12 Baches St., London, N.1.

CZECHOSLOVAKIA: Boosey & Hawkes, 295 Regent St., London, W.1.

DENMARK: J. & W. Chester, 7 Eagle Court, London, E.C.1.

FRANCE: United Music Publishers, 1 Montague St., London, W.1.

GERMANY: Hinrichsen, *see above.*
Novello, 1-3 Upper James St., London, W.1.
Schott, 48 Gt. Marlborough St., London, W.1.

HOLLAND: Lengnick, Purley Oak Studios, 421a Brighton Rd., S. Croydon.

HUNGARY: Boosey & Hawkes, *see above.*

ISRAEL: Chester, *see above.*

ITALY: { Hinrichsen, *see above.*
{ Ricordi, The Bury, Church St., Chesham, Bucks.

NORWAY: { Chester, *see above.*
{ Hinrichsen, *see above.*

POLAND: Musica Rara, 2 Gt. Marlborough St. London, W.1.

RUSSIA: Musica Rara, *see above.*

SWEDEN: { Chester, *see above.*
{ Hinrichsen, *see above.*

SWITZERLAND: Hinrichsen, *see above.*

U.S.A.: { Boosey & Hawkes, *see above.*
{ Hinrichsen, *see above.*
{ Mills Music, 20 Denmark St., London, W.C.2.
{ Schott, *see above.*

MUSICA RARA specialize in wind music, and in addition to keeping a large stock they will gladly undertake to trace works ordered.

BASSOON AND ORCHESTRA

BACH, J. C.	Concerto in B♮ major	*Sikorski*
	,, E♮ major	,,
BERWALD, J. F.	Concertstück Op. 2	*MS, Stockholm*
BITSCH, MARCEL	Concertino	*Leduc*
BODART, EUGEN	Concerto in E♮ major	*Müller, Heidelberg*
BOISMORTIER, J. B. DE (arr. Oubradous)	Concerto in D major	*SEMl, Paris*

BOND, CAPEL	Concerto in B♭		Boosey & Hawkes
BOZZA, EUGENE	Concertino	Op. 49	Leduc
BRUNS, VICTOR	Concerto No. 1	Op. 5	Breitkopf
	Concerto No. 2	Op. 15	Hofmeister
DANZI, FRANZ	3 Concertos		MS, Donaueschingen
DAVID, FERD.	Concertino	Op. 12	Kistner
DEVIENNE, F.	Concerto in C		Hofmeister
DONATONI, FRANCO	Concerto (1952)		Drago, Milan
ELGAR, EDWARD	Romance	Op. 62	Novello
ERIKSSON, NILS	Concerto (1949)		FST, Stockholm
FASCH, J. F.	Concerto		Noetzel, Wilhelms-haven
FELD, JINDŘICH	Concerto (1961)		Leduc
FERNSTRÖM, J.	Concerto		FST, Stockholm
FOGG, ERIC	Concerto		Elkin
GRAUN, J. G.	Concerto in B♭		Sikorski
GRAUPNER, CHRISTOPH	Concerto in C minor		Bärenreiter
GRØNDAHL, LAUNY	Concerto (1942)		SUDM, Copenhagen
HENNEBERG, A.	Concerto		FST, Stockholm
HUMMEL, J. F.	Concertstück	Op. 201	Breitkopf
HUMMEL, J. N.	Concerto		MS, London
JACOB, GORDON	Concerto		Williams
JOLIVET, ANDRÉ	Concerto		Heugel
KELEMEN, MILKO	Concerto		UE
KOZELUCH, JOH. ANTON	Concerto		MS, Prague, Russian State
LANDOWSKI, M.	Concerto		Choudens
LARSSEN, LARS ERIK	Concertino		Gehrmann, Sweden
LOUEL, J.	Burlesque (1943)		Cebedem
LUTYENS, ELIZ.	Concerto Grosso	Op. 83	Chester
MACONCHY, ELIZ.	Concertino		Lengnick

MAESSEN, A.	Divertimento (1960)		*Donemus*
MAINGUENEAU, L.	Suite brève		*Durand*
MARESCOTTI, A. F.	Fantaisie, Giboulées		*Jobert*
MAROS, RUDOLF	Concertino		*Musica, Budapest*
MATZ, A.	Concerto		*Breitkopf*
MEISTER, KARL	Concerto		*Ars viva*
MEULEMANS, A.	Rhapsodie (1942)		*Cebedem*
MOZART, W. A.	Concerto	K. 191	*Breitkopf*
	Concerto	KA. 230a	*Peters, Litolff*
MÜLLER, S. W.	Concerto	Op. 56	*Eulenburg*
PAUER, JIRI	Concerto		*Artia, Prague*
PHILLIPS, BURRILL	Concert Piece		*Carl Fischer*
PIERNÉ, GABRIEL	Solo de Concert		*Leduc*
ROSETTI, F.A. (RÖSSLER)	Concerto in B♭		*Schott*
SPISAK, MICHEL	Concerto		*Ricordi*
STAMITZ, KARL	Concerto in F		*Sikorski, Schott*
THILMAN, J. P.	Sonatine		*Hofmeister*
	Concerto		„
TOMASI, HENRI	Concerto		*Leduc*
VIVALDI, A.	19 Concertos		*Ricordi*
WEBER, C. M. VON	Concerto in F	Op. 75	*Lienau*
	Introduction & Rondo	Op. 35	„
WHETTAM, GRAHAM	Concerto a Capriccio Op.22		*De Wolfe*
WOLF-FERRARI, ERMANNO	Suite-Concertino		*Ricordi*

SOLO INSTRUMENTS AND ORCHESTRA

BECK, C.	Concertino for cl, bn	*Schott*
BEETHOVEN, L. VAN	Romance for fl, bn pf	*Breitkpof*
BLACHER, B.	Concerto for cl, bn, hn, trb	*Bote & Bock*
DANZI, F.	Sinfonia Concertante for fl, ob, hn, bn	*Schott*

ECKHARDT- GRAMATTÉ, S.	Triple Concerto for cl, bn, trp	*UE*
GALLON, NOËL	Concerto for ob, cl, bn	*Leduc*
HAYDN, J.	Sinfonia Concertante for ob, bn, vn, vc	*Breitkopf*
HINDEMITH, P.	Concerto for bn, trp Concerto for fl, cor ang, cl, bn	*Schott* ,,
HOLBROOKE, J.	Quadruple Concerto for fl, ob, cl, bn	*De Wolfe*
MACONCHY, ELIZ.	Duo-Concertante for ob, bn	*Lengnick*
MOZART, W. A.	Sinfonia Concertante for ob, cl, hn, bn K. 297b	*Breitkopf*
RIETI, VITTORIO	Concerto for quintet	*UE*
SAEVERUD, HARALD	Rondo Amoroso for ob, bn	*Mills*
SCHNEIDER, G. A.	Sinfonia Concertante for cl, bn Op. 89	*Bote & Bock*
STAMITZ, A.	Sinfonia Concertante for ob, bn	*Kneusslin*
STAMITZ, K.	Double Concerto for cl, bn	*Sikorski*
STRAUSS, R.	Duett-Concertino for cl, bn	*Boosey & Hawkes*
WANHAL, J. B.	Concerto for 2bn	*Hofmeister*

BASSOON AND PIANO

ANDRÉ-THIRIET, A. L.	Thème et Variations (1954)		*Leduc*
ANTJUFJEV, B.	2 Pieces (1954)	Op. 83	*Russian State*
BAINES, FRANCIS	Intro & Hornpipe		*Schott*
BAIRD, TADEUSZ	4 Preludes (1954)		*Polish State*
BAKALEINIKOFF, VLADIMIR	3 Pieces		*Belwin Inc.*
BALANTSCHIVADSE, AND.	Concertino (1954)		*Russian State*
BARILLER, ROBERT	Fantasio (1960)		*Leduc*

E

BEEKHUIS, H.	Sonatine	*Donemus*
BEN-HAIM, P.	3 Songs without Words	*Israel M.P.*
BERGHMANS, J.	Les Oursons Savants (1958)	*Leduc*
BERGMANN, W.	Prelude & Fugue	*Schott*
BERNIER, R.	Bassonerie	*Leduc*
BERTELIN, A.	Intro & Rondo (1905)	*Evette*
BERTONI, U.	Concerto	*Bongiovanni*
	Capriccio	*Ricordi*
BESOZZI, GIROLAMO	Sonata	*O.U.P.*
BINET, JEAN	Variations	*Henn, Geneva*
BITSCH, MARCEL	Concertino (1948)	*Leduc*
	Rondoletto	*,,*
	Passepied	*P. Noël*
BLOCH, ANDRE	Fantaisie variée	*Leduc*
	Dancing Jack	*Fougères*
	Goguenardises	*P. Noël*
BLOMDAHL, KARL BIRGER	Little Suite (1945)	*FST, Stockholm*
BOISMORTIER, J. B. DE	Sonata No. 5	*Siècle Musicale, Geneva*
BONNARD, G.	Sonata (1937)	*Ricordi*
BOSSI, M. ENRICO	Improvviso	*Pizzi, Bologna*
	Feuillets d'album	*Rieter-Biedermann*
BOURDEAU, E.	Solos Nos. 1–3	*Leduc*
BOURGAULT-DUCOUDRAY, L.A.	Fantaisie	*Evette*
BOUSSAGOL, E.	Serenade	*,,*
BOZZA, EUGENE	Recitative, Sicilienne & Rondo	*Leduc*
	Burlesque	*,,*
	Fantaisie (1945)	*,,*
	Espieglerie	*,,*
	Duettino	*,,*
BRUNS, VICTOR	Sonata Op. 20	*Pro Musica*

BÜSSER, HENRI	Récit & Thème varié Op. 37	*Leduc*
	Pièce de concours Op. 66	„
	Cantilène & Rondo Op. 75	„
	Portuguesa Op. 106	„
BÜTTNER, MAX	Improvisationen Op. 22	*Hofmeister*
CADOW, P.	Variations (1941)	*Grosch, Würzburg*
CASADESUS, ROBERT	2 Pièces (1961)	*Durand*
CASCARINO, ROMEO	Sonata (1950)	*Arrow Music Press, New York*
CHALLAN, HENRI	Suite	*Selmer*
CHAPUIS, A.	Fantaisie concertante	*Durand*
CHILDS, BARNEY	Sonata (1938)	*C.C.C., New York*
CLÉRISSE, ROBERT	Thème de Concours	*Leduc*
COENEN, J. M.	Sonata (1864)	*Weygand, den Haag*
COHN, ARTHUR	Declamation & Toccata	*Elkan-Vogel*
	Hebraic Study	„
COLACO OSORIO-SWAAB R.	Cavatina	*Donemus*
	Sonatina	„
COOLS, EUGENE	Concertstück Op. 80	*Evette*
COUPREVITCH, V.	Scherzino	*Russian State*
DALLIER, HENRI	Sonata in B♭	*Evette*
DAMASE, JEAN MICHEL	Aria Op. 7	*Salabert*
DECRUCK, F.	Scherzo fantasque	*Selmer*
DE LAMARTER, ERIC	Folksong, Scherzetto (1950)	*Witmark*
	Arietta (1950)	„
DELAUNAY, R.	Scherzando	*Selmer*
DELCROIX	Prelude & Caprice	*Evette*
DEMERSSEMAN, J.	Introduction & Polonaise Op. 30	*Costallat*
DEMUTH, NORMAN	Sonata (1955)	*MS*
DESPORTES, Y.	Chanson d'Antan	*Leduc*
DOMENICO, O. DI	Sonatina	„
DOMINSCHEN, K.	Scherzo	*Russian State*

DUBOIS, P. M.	Sérénades		*Leduc*
	Virelai (1961)		,,
DUBRUCQ, EDWARD	Humoresque		*Mahillon*
DUCLOS, RENÉ	Fagottino		*Leduc*
	3 Nocturnes		,,
	Quadrille		*P. Noël*
DUNHILL, THOMAS	Lyric Suite	Op. 96	*Boosey & Hawkes*
	Intermezzo		*Williams*
DUTILLEUX, HENRI	Sarabande & Cortège		*Leduc*
DVARIONAS, B.	Thème & Vars. (1952)		*Russian State*
ELGAR, EDWARD	Romance	Op. 62	*Novello*
ESSEX, KENNETH	Suite (1952)		*MS*
ETLER, ALVIN	Sonata (1955)		*AMP*
FALCINELLI, ROLANDE	Berceuse (1956)		*Leduc*
FINKELSTEIN, I. B.	3 Concert pieces (1958)		*CK, Leningrad*
FLAMENT, EDUARD	Concertstück		*Evette*
FORET, FELICIEN	Prelude, Aria & Fugue		*Costallat*
	Pièces brèves (1938)		*Buffet*
FOSTER, IVOR	2 Simple Pieces	Op. 10	*Williams*
GABAYE, P.	Toccatina		*Leduc*
GAGNEBIN, HENRI	Scherzetto		,,
GALLIARD, J. E.	6 Sonatas		*McGinnis & Marx*
	Suite No. 1, arr. A. Camden		*Mills*
	Suite No. 2, arr. A. Camden		,,
GALLOIS-MONTBRUN, RENÉ	Improvisation		*Leduc*
GALLON, NOËL	Recitative & Allegro (1939)		*Oiseau Lyre*
GEDDA, GIULIO C.	Sonata Umoristica		*Genovese, Turin*
GEISER, WALTER	Capriccio	Op. 33	*Bärenreiter*
GLIÉRE, REINHOLD	2 Pieces Op. 35.8, 9		*IMC, Jurgenson*
GOEPFART, KARL	2 Charakterstücke	Op. 31	*Hofmeister*
GÓRECKI, B.	Etiuda Nr. 1		*Czytelnik, Poland*
GRIMM, F. K.	Sonata	Op. 113	*Wrede*

GROVLEZ, GABRIEL Sicilienne & Allegro giocoso *Leduc*
Sarabande & Allegro *Costallat*

GUIDE, RICHARD DE Élégie et Consolation (1958)
Op. 32.2. *Leduc*

GUILLOU, RENÉ Ballade *Gras, Paris*

HAAN, STEFAN DE Scherzo *Schott*

HALSEY, LOUIS Sonata

HENNESSY, SWAN Pièce Celtique Op. 74 *Eschig*

HILMERA, OLDRICH Con Umore: 3 Pieces *Hudebni Matice, Prague*

HINDEMITH, PAUL Sonata *Schott*

HLOBIL, EMIL Divertimento Op. 29 *Artia, Prague*

HURLSTONE,
 WILLIAM Y. Sonata in F *Cary*

IBERT, JACQUES Carignane *P. Noël*

JACOBI, CARL Intro & Polonaise Op. 9 *Schott*
Variations *Pro Musica*

JANCOURT, EUGEN 18 Solos, etc. *Costallat, etc.*

JEANJEAN, PAUL Prelude & Scherzo (1911) *Leduc*

JELESCU, P. Rapsodie dobrogeana(1956) *Rumanian State*

KARDSAS, J. Suite (1959) *Russian State*

KERRISON, JAN 3 Young Pieces *Mills*
Suite of Dances *Mills*

KESNAR, M. Concerto (1954) *Cundy-Bettoney*

KOECHLIN, CHAS. 3 Pieces Op. 34 *MS, Paris*
Sonata Op. 71 *MS, Paris*

KOHS, ELLIS B. Sonatina (1953) *Merrymount Music Press*

KORTCHMAROFF Esquisse (1924) *Russian State*

KOSTIC, D. Sonatina *Muzick Naklada, Zagreb*

LABATE, BRUNO Humoresque (1948) *Alfred Music Co., New York*

LAJTHA, LASZLO Intermezzo *Leduc*

LANGE, HANS Suite (1940) Op. 17 *Lange, Berlin*

LANTIER, PIERRE	Danse Bouffonne (1949)		Leduc
LAVAGNE, P.	Steeple-Chase		P. Noël
LECAIL	Fant. concertant		Leduc
LISTE, ANTOINE	Sonata in F	Op. 3	Costallat
LONGO, ALESSANDRO	Suite (1915)	Op. 69	Ricordi
LUCAS, LEIGHTON	Orientale		Chester
MAINGUENEAU, LOUIS	Suite brève		Durand
MAIXANDEAU	Lied & Rondo		Leduc
MARESCOTTI, F. A.	Fantaisie, Giboulées		Jobert
MARKIEWICZOWNA, W.	Toccata		Polish State
MARTELLI, HENRI	Thème varié	Op. 74	Eschig
	Sonata		Philippo, Paris
MAUGÜÉ, J. M. L.	Divertissements Champêtres		Costallat
MAZELLIER, JULES	Prelude & Danse		Leduc
MERCI, LUIDGI	Sonata in G minor		Schott
MIGNON, EDMOND	Sonata (1954)		Mignon
MIHAILOVICI, MARCEL	Novelette		Leduc
	Sonate	Op. 76	Heugel
MILDE, LUDWIG	Andante & Rondo	Op. 25	Lienau
	Tarantelle	Op. 20	Russian State
MONFEUILLARD	Lamento & Final		Philippo, Paris
MORITZ, EDUARD	Scherzo		Zimmermann
MORTARI, VIRGILIO	Marche Fériale		Leduc
MOSER, RUDOLF	Suite	Op. 97	MS, Basel
MOUQUET, JULES	Ballade (1912)	Op. 34	Evette
MULDBR, H.	Sonata No. 5	Op. 54	Donemus
NICOLOV, LAZAR	2 Pieces (1951)		Bulgarian State
NUSSIO, OTMAR	Variazioni		UE
OLLONE, MAX D'	Romance & Tarantelle (1922)		Leduc

ORBAN, MAURICE	Sonate	*Costallat*
OREFICE, A.	Adagio	*Evette*
OUBRADOUS, FERNAND	Récit & Variations (1938)	*Leduc*
	Cadence & Divertissement	*Oiseau Lyre*
	Divertissement	*P. Noël*
OZI, ETIENNE	Grande Sonate	*Siècle Musicale, Geneva*
	Adagio & Rondo	,, ,,
PACIORKIEWICZ, TADEUSZ	Sonatina (1956)	*Polish State*
PAUER, JIRI	Capriccio	*Artia, Prague*
PETIT, P.	Guilledoux	*Leduc*
PIANTONI, LUIGI	Pastorale & Rondeau (1943)	*Conservatoire de Genève*
PIERNÉ, GABRIEL	Solo de Concert Op. 35	*Leduc*
	Prélude de Concert Op. 53	*Salabert*
PIERNÉ, PAUL	Thème & Variations (1941)	*Costallat*
POOT, MARCEL	Ballade	*Leduc*
PRESLE, J. DE LA	Petite Suite	,,
	Orientale	,,
PUGET, PAUL	Solo de basson (1899)	,,
RAKOV, NIKOLAI	Etude (1956)	*Russian State*
RAPHAËL, GUENTER	Berceuse (1959)	*Leduc*
RATEZ, E.	Impromptu Op. 67	*Andrieu, Paris*
	Variations Op. 72	*Hamelle*
RATHAUS, KAROL	Polichinelle	*Belwin Inc.*
REICHA, ANTOINE	Sonate	*MS, Paris*
REUTTER, H.	Sérénade (1957)	*Leduc*
REVEL, P.	Petite Suite	,,
RENÉ, CHARLES	Solo de Concert	*Lemoine*
ROSCHER, JOSEF	Andante & Allegretto Op. 81	*Schott*
	12 Vortragsstücke Op. 88	,,
RUTHENFRANZ, ROBERT	Divertimento (1960)	*Metropolis, Antwerp*

SAINT-SAËNS, CAMILLE	Sonate	Op. 168	*Durand*
SAUGUET, HENRI	Barcarolle		*Ed. Sociales Internationales, Paris*
SCHAFER, C.	Capriccio		*Zimmermann*
SCHAEFERS, A.	Capriccio		*Sikorski*
SCHMID, H. K.	Ode	Op. 34.3	*Schott*
SCHOECK, OTHMAR	Sonata (orig. bcl)	Op. 41	*Breitkopf*
SCHOLLUM, ROBERT	Sonatine	Op. 55.3	*Doblinger*
SCHOUWMAN, H.	Romanze & Humoresque Op. 33		*Donemus*
SCHRECK, GUSTAV	Sonata	Op. 9	*Hofmeister*
SEMLER-COLLÈRY, JULES	Récitatif & Final		*Eschig*
SENAILLÉ, J. B.	Intro & Allegro spiritoso (arr.)		*Goodwin & Tabb*
SKALKOTTAS, N.	Sonate Concertante Op. 67		*MS, Athens*
SPOHR, LOUIS	Adagio in F	Op. 115	*Schott*
STADIO CIRO	Serenata		*Ricordi*
	Burlesca		,,
STEKEL, E. P.	Mélodie (1953)		*Leduc*
STEVENS, HALSEY	3 Pieces		*Hinrichsen*
STOLTE, S.	Spielmusik (1957)		*Peters*
SUCHANEK	Concertino (1948)		*Russian State*
TAK, P. C.	Vars. (1944)		*Donemus*
TANNER, PETER	Sonata (1956)		*Tanner*
TANSMAN, ALEX.	Sonatine		*Eschig*
TAUDOU, A.	Morceau de Concours (1904)		*Evette*
TELEMANN, G. P.	Sonata in F minor		*IMC, New York*
THILMAN, J. P.	Sonatine		*Hofmeister*
THIRIET, A. L.	Thème & Vars.		*Leduc*
TILLMETZ, RUDOLF	Romanze & Burleske Op. 37		*Rahter*

TOMASI, HENRI	Danse Guerrière (1960)	*Leduc*
TSCHEMBERDJY, N.	Humoresque (1936)	*Russian State*
TSCHEREPNIN, NICOLAI	Variations simples (1935)	*Schirmer*
	Esquisse	Op. 45.7 *Chester*
VIDAL, PAUL	Adagio & Saltarelle (1929)	*Leduc*
	Mélodie	,,
VINTER, GILBERT	The Playful Pachyderm	*Boosey & Hawkes*
	Reverie	*Cramer*
VLADIGUEROV, PANTCHO	Caprice (1951)	*Bulgarian State*
WEINBERGER, JAROMIR	Sonatine (1940)	*Carl Fischer*
WEISSENBORN, JULIUS	Romanze	Op. 3 *Forberg*
	6 Vortragsstücke	Op. 9 ,,
	3 Vortragsstücke	Op. 10 *Breitkopf*
	Capriccio	Op. 14 *Hofmeister*
WICHTL, ANTON M.	Concerto (1911)	Op. 2 *Hawkes*
WLASSOW, V. & FEHRE V.	4 Pieces (1932)	*Russian State*
ZBINDEN, J. F.	Ballade	Op. 33 *Breitkopf*
ZINSSTAG, DOLF	Elégie	*Henn, Geneva*

BASSOONS ONLY

ALFVEN, HUGO	Trio	*Gehrmann, Sweden*
ALMENRÄDER, KARL	Duo	Op. 8 *Spratt*
APOSTEL, H. E.	Sonatine Op. 19.3 (solo)	*UE*
BANTOCK, GRANVILLE	Dance of the Witches (trio)	*Swan*
	The Witches' Frolic (trio)	*Goodwin & Tabb*
BENTZON, J.	Studies in variation form. Op. 34 (solo)	*Skandinavisk, Copenhagen*
BERGT, ADOLPH	Trio	*Hofmeister*
BLUME, O.	12 Duets	*Fischer*

E*

BOISMORTIER, J. B. DE	5 Sonaten		*Moeck, Celle*
BOZZA, EUGENE	Divertissements (trio)		*Leduc*
,,	Duettino		*Leduc*
CORNETTE, VICTOR	18 Duos		*Costallat*
COUPERIN, FRANÇOIS	13me Concert (duo)		*Oiseau Lyre*
DHERIN, G.	16 Variations (solo)		*Eschig*
DOTZAUER, J. J. F.	3 Duos Concertants Op. 10		*Peters*
DUBENSKY, A.	Prelude & Fugue (quartet) (1938)		*Ricordi*
ENOSKO-BOROWSKI, A.	Scherzo (trio)	Op. 13	*Russian State*
ERBACH, F. C.	6 Duos (1954)		*Bärenreiter*
FUCHS, G. F.	6 Trios		*Lemoine*
HAAN, S. DE	Suite (trio)		*Hinrichsen*
HOLLAND, THEODORE	Cortège (quartet)		,,
JANCOURT, E.	9 Sonatas (duo), etc.		*Costallat*
KUMMER, G. H.	Trios		*Hofmeister*
MANCINELLI, DOMENICO	2 Sonatas (duo)		*Ricordi*
MOORTEL, A. VAN DE	Partita (solo)	Op. 1	*Moortel, Brussels*
MULDER, ERNST	Trio (1942)		*Donemus*
MÜLLER, P.	35 Duets		*Spratt*
OZI, ETIENNE	3 kleine Sonaten (duo)		*Hofmeister*
PROKOFIEV, S.	Scherzo Humoristique		*Forberg*
SCHUMAN, WILLIAM	Quartettino		*Rongwen Inc.*
WELLESZ, EGON	Suite (solo)	Op. 77	*Rongwen Music, New York.*

CHAMBER MUSIC FOR BASSOON AND STRINGS

BAX, ARNOLD	Threnody & Scherzo for bn, hp, str quintet	*MS, Chappell*

DANZI, FRANZ	Quartet for bn, str trio	
	Op. 40.3 *M Rara*	
DEVIENNE, FRANÇOIS	Quartet for bn, str trio	
	Op. 73.1 *M Rara*	
FLAMENT, EDUARD	Fantaisie for bn, vn, vc	
	Op. 54 *Evette*	
FRANÇAIX, JEAN	Quintet for bn, str quartet	*MS, Paris*
GAL, HANS	Divertissement for bn, vc	*MS, Edinburgh*
HINDEMITH, PAUL	Stücke for bn, vc (1942)	*MS*
HOLBROOKE, JOSEF	Quintet for bn, str quartet	
	Op. 134 *MS, London*	
LANGE, HANS	Quintet for bn, str quartet *Lange, Berlin* (1937)	
MOZART, W. A.	Sonata for bn, vc K292	*Breitkopf, Ö.B.V.,etc*
OZI, ETIENNE	6 Sonatas for bn, vc	*Afranius, Berne*
ROUSSEL, ALBERT	Duo for bn, cb	*Durand*
SATTER, GUSTAV	Sextet for bn, 2vn, va, 2vc (1869) Op. 109 *Forberg*	
SEARLE, HUMPHREY	Variations for bn, str quartet *MS, Williams*	
SPISAK, MICHEL	Duo for bn, va	*Ricordi*
VILLA-LOBOS, HEITOR	Quintet for bn, str quartet *MS*	

MISCELLANEOUS CHAMBER MUSIC

ANDRIESSEN, HENDRIK	Quintet	*Donemus*
ARNOLD, MALCOLM	Trio for fl, bn, va	*Lengnick*
	3 Shanties for quintet	*Paterson*
ARRIEU, CLAUDE	Trio	*Amphion*
AURIC, GEORGE	Trio	*Oiseau Lyre*
BACH, C. P. E.	6 Sonatas for cl, bn, pf	*Bärenreiter*
	6 Sonatas for 2fl, 2cl, 2hn, bn	*M Rara*

BACH, J. C.	4 Quints, 2cl, 2hn, bn	*Boosey & Hawkes*
	3 Marches for 2ob, 2hn, bn	*Sikorski*
	Symphonies for 2cl, 2hn, bn	*Hofmeister*
BARBER, SAMUEL	Summer Music for quintet Op. 31	*Schirmer*
BARTHE, ADOLPHE	Passacaille for quintet	*Leduc*
BARTOS, F.	Suite 'le bourgeois Gentil-homme' for quintet	*Artia, Prague*
BEETHOVEN, L. VAN	3 Duos for cl, bn	*Breitkopf, etc.*
	Trio for fl, bn, pf	*Breitkopf, IMC, New York*
	Quintet for ob, cl, hn, bn, pf Op. 16	*Breitkopf*
	Quintet for ob, 3hn, bn	*Schott*
	Sextet for 2cl, 2bn, 2hn Op. 71	*Breitkopf*
	Septet for cl. hn, bn, vn, va, vc, cb Op. 20	*Peters, etc.*
	Octet for 2ob, 2cl, 2bn, 2hn Op. 103	*Breitkopf*
	Rondino for 2ob, 2cl, 2bn, 2hn	,,
BERWALD, J. F.	Septet for cl, hn, bn, vn, va, vc, cb	*FST, Stockholm*
BOCCHERINI, LUIGI	Sextet for ob, bn, str qt	*Hofmeister*
	Sextet for ob, hn, bn, vn, va, vc Op. 42.2	*Sikorski*
BÖDDECKER, PHILIPP F.	Sonata sopra la Monica for vn, bn, cont	*Kistner & Siegel*
BOZZA, EUGENE	Sonatine for fl, bn	*Leduc*
BRIDGE, FRANK	Divertimento for fl, ob, cl, bn	*Boosey & Hawkes*
BUSH, GEOFFRY	Trio for ob, bn, pf	*Augener*
CASELLA, ALFREDO	Serenata for cl, bn, trp, vn, vc	*UE*
CHABRIER, E.	L'invitation au voyage for voice, bn, pf	*Costallat*

CORRETTE, MICHEL Concerto 'le phénix' for *Siècle mus., Geneva*
4bn, clavecin

DAMASE,
  JEAN MICHEL 17 Variations for quintet *Leduc*

DANZI, FRANZ Quintet Op. 56.1 *Leuckart*
Op. 56.2 ,,
Op. 67.2 *Hinrichsen, Kneusslin*
Quintet for ob, cl, hn, bn, *M Rara*
pf

DITTERSDORF 3 Partiten for 2ob, 2hn, bn *Breitkopf*
Parthia for 2ob, 2hn, bn *M Rara*
Divertimento for 2ob, 2cl, *Sikorski*
bn

DVOŘÁK, ANTONIN Serenade for 2ob, 2cl, 3hn,
2bn, va, vc Op. 44 *Simrock, M Rara*

FASCH, J. F. Sonata for 2ob, bn *Sikorski*
Sonata for 2ob, bn, pf *Sikorski*

FERGUSON,
  HOWARD Octet for cl, hn, bn, str qt, *Boosey & Hawkes*
cb

FRANÇAIX, J. Divertissement for trio *Schott*
Quartet for fl, ob, cl, bn ,,
Quintet ,,

FRICKER,
  PETER RACINE Quintet Op. 5 ,,

GALLON, NOËL Sonate for fl, bn *Leduc*

GEBAUER, J. 6 Duos for cl, bn Op. 8 *Sikorski*
6 Duos for fl, bn Op. 22 *Costallat*

GERHARD,
  ROBERTO Quintet *Mills*

GLINKA, M. Trio Pathétique for cl, bn, *Jurgenson, M Rara*
pf

GOEPFART, K. E. Quartet for fl, ob, hn, bn
Op. 93 *Schuberth*

GOEPFERT, C. A. 6 Duos faciles for cl, bn *Hofmeister*

GOUNOD, CHARLES Petite Symphonie for fl, *Costallat*
2ob, 2cl, 2bn, 2hn

GRAINGER, PERCY	Walking Tune for quintet	*Schott*
HAAN, STEFAN DE	Divertimento for cl, bn	*Hinrichsen*
	Trio for fl, cl, bn	*Schott*
HAYDN, JOSEPH	Divertimento arr. for quintet	*Boosey & Hawkes*
	Octet for 2ob, 2cl, 2bn, 2hn	*Bote & Bock*
	2 Sextets for 2ob, 2hn, 2bn	*M Rara*
	Sextet for ob, hn, bn, vn, va, vc	,,
HAYDN, MICHAEL	Divertimento for fl, ob, cl, bn	*Hofmeister*
HENZE, H. W.	Quintet	*Schott*
HERTEL, J. W.	Sonata for 2hn, 2bn	*Noetzel, Wilhelms-haven*
HINDEMITH, PAUL	Kleine Kammermusik for quintet Op. 24.2	*Schott*
	Septet for fl, ob, cl, bcl, bn, hn, trp	,,
	Octet for cl, hn, bn, vn, 2va, vc	,,
IBERT, JACQUES	5 Pièces en trio	*Oiseau Lyre*
	2 Mouvements for 2fl, cl, bn	*Leduc*
	3 Pièces brèves for quintet	,,
JACOB, GORDON	Suite for quintet	*MS, London*
	Sextet for quintet, pf	*M Rara*
	Serenade for 2fl, 2ob, 2cl, 2bn	
JANÁČEK, LEOS	Mladi Suite for fl, ob, cl, bcl, hn, bn	*Hudebni Matice, Prague*
	Concertino for cl, hn, bn, 2vn, va, pf	*Artia, Prague*
JOLIVET, ANDRÉ	Pastorales de Noel for fl, bn, hp	*Heugel*
KLUGHARDT, AUGUST F. M.	Quintet Op. 79	*Zimmermann*
KOECHLIN, CHARLES	Trio for fl, cl, bn	*Salabert*
	Septet for fl, ob, cor ang, cl, sax, hn, bn	*Oiseau Lyre*

KREUTZER, CONRADIN	Trio for cl, bn, pf Op. 43	*Hofmeister*
	Septet for cl, hn, bn, vn, va, vc, cb Op. 62	*M Rara*
LEFEBVRE, CHARLES	Suite for quintet Op. 57	*Hamelle*
	Suite No. 2 for quintet	*Evette*
MAGNARD, ALBÉRIC	Quintet for fl, ob, cl, bn, pf Op. 8	*Salabert*
MALIPIERO, G. F.	Epodi e Giambi for ob, bn, vn, va	*Hansen*
	Sonata a 4 for fl, ob, cl, bn	*UE*
MARKEVITCH, IGOR	Serenade for cl, bn, vn	*Schott*
MARTINU, BOHUSLAV	4 Madrigals for trio	,,
	La Revue de Cuisine for cl, bn, trp, vn, vc, pf	*Leduc*
MILHAUD, DARIUS	Suite d'après Corette for trio	*Oiseau Lyre*
	Pastorale for trio	*Chant du monde*
	La Cheminée du roi René for quintet	*Andraud*
	2 Sketches for quintet	*Mercury Music*
MORITZ, EDUARD	Quintet	*Zimmermann*
	Div. for fl, cl, bn	,,
MOZART, W. A.	5 Divertimenti for 2cl, bn KA229	*Breitkopf*
	Canonic Adagio for 2basset-hn, bn K410	,,
	6 Divertimenti for 2ob, 2hn, 2bn	,,
	Quintet for ob, cl, hn, bn, pf K452	*Bärenreiter, Breitkopf, M Rara*
	Divertimento for 2hn, bn, vn, va, vc K205	*Breitkopf*
	Sextet for 2cl, 2hn, 2bn K375	*Schott, M Rara*
	2 Serenades for 2ob, 2cl, 2hn, 2bn K375, 388	*Breitkopf, M Rara*

MOZART, W. A. *(continued)*	Octet for 2ob, 2cl, 2hn, 2bn K196f	*Schott*
	2 Divertimenti for 2ob, 2cor ang, 2cl, 2hn, 2bn K166, 186	*Breitkopf*
	Serenade for 2ob, 2cl, 2 basset hn, 4hn, 2bn, cbn K361	*Breitkopf, M Rara*
MÜLLER, PETER	Quintet	*M Rara*
NAUMANN, J. G.	Duets for ob, bn	*Sikorski*
NIELSEN, CARL	Serenata invano for cl, hn, bn, vc, cb	*Skandinavisk, Copenhagen*
	Quintet Op. 43	*Hansen*
ONSLOW, GEORGE	Quintet Op. 81	*Leuckart*
PIERNÉ, GABRIEL	Pastorale for quintet Op. 14	*Leduc*
PIJPER, WILLIAM	Trio for fl, cl, bn	*Donemus*
	Quintet	,,
	Sextet for quintet, pf	,,
	Septet for quintet, cb, pf	,,
PITFIELD, THOMAS	Trio for ob, bn, pf	*Augener*
POOT, MARCEL	Octet for cl, hn, bn, str qt, cb	*Cebedem*
POULENC, FRANCIS	Sonata for cl, bn	*Chester*
	Trio for ob, bn, pf	*Hansen*
	Sextet for quintet, pf	,,
REICHA, ANTOINE	24 Quintets	*Simrock, Costallat*
	3 Quintets	*Artia, Prague*
	2 Quintets Op. 88.2, 88.5	*Leuckart*
	2 Quintets Op. 91.3, 100.3	*Kneusslin*
REIZENSTEIN, FRANZ	Quintet	*Boosey & Hawkes*
RIMSKY-KORSAKOV, N.	Quintet for fl, cl, hn, bn, pf	*IMC, New York*
ROLAND-MANUEL	Suite dans le goût espagnol for ob, bn, trp, pf	*Leduc*
ROSSINI, G.	6 Quartets for fl, cl, hn, bn	*Schott*

ROUSSEL, ALBERT	Divertissement for quintet, pf	*Salabert*
RUBINSTEIN, ANTON	Quintet for fl, cl, hn, bn, pf Op. 55	*Schuberth*
SAUGUET, HENRI	Trio	*Oiseau Lyre*
SAUNDERS, MAX	Trio for fl, bn, va	*Ricordi*
SCHMID, H. K.	Quintet Op. 28	*Schott*
SCHMITT, FLORENT	A Tours d'anches for ob, cl, bn, pf	*Durand*
SCHÖNBERG, ARNOLD	Quintet Op. 26	*UE*
SCHUBERT, FRANZ	Octet for cl, hn, bn, str qt, cb Op. 166	*Peters, etc.*
	Menuett & Finale for 2ob, 2cl, 2hn, 2bn	*Breitkopf*
SEARLE, HUMPHREY	Quartet for cl, bn, vn, va Op. 12	*Hinrichsen*
SEIBER, MATYAS	Serenade for 2cl, 2bn, 2hn	*Hansen*
	Quintet	*Schott*
SPITZMÜLLER, A.	Divertimento breve for bn, 2vn, va, pf Op. 6	*UE*
SPOHR, LOUIS	Quintet for fl, cl, hn, bn, pf Op. 52	*Bärenreiter*
	Septet for fl, cl, hn, bn, vn, vc, pf Op. 147	*Peters*
	Nonet for quintet, vn, va, vc, cb Op. 31	,,
STAMITZ, KARL	Quartet for ob, cl, hn, bn Op. 82	*Leuckart*
STRAUSS, RICHARD	Serenade for 2fl, 2ob, 2cl, 4hn, 2bn, cbn Op.7	*UE, IMC, New York*
STRAVINSKY, IGOR	Pastorale for ob, cor ang, cl, bn, vn	*Schott*
	Septet for cl. hn, bn, vn, va, vc, pf	*Boosey & Hawkes*
	Octet for fl, cl, 2bn, 2trp, 2trb	,, ,,

SZALOWSKY, ANTON	Divertimento for trio	*Chester*
TAFFANEL, PAUL	Quintet	*Leduc*
TELEMANN, G. P.	Suite for 2ob, 2hn, bn	*Leuckart*
	Suite No. 2 for 2ob, 2hn, bn	*Hinrichsen*
TOMASI, HENRI	Concert Champêtre for trio	*Leduc*
	Quintet	,,
	Variations for quintet	,,
VILLA-LOBOS, HEITOR	Bachianas Brasilieras No. 6 for fl, bn	*AMP*
	Trio	*Eschig*
	Fantasie Concertant for cl, bn, pf	,,
	Quartet for fl, ob, cl, bn	,,
	Quintette en forme de choros for fl, ob, cor ang, cl, bn	,,
	Choros No. 7 for fl, ob, cl, sax, bn, vn, pf	,,
VIVALDI, ANTONIO	Sonata for fl, bn, cont	*Ricordi*
	Concerto for fl, ob, bn	*Ricordi*
	Concerto for fl, ob, vn, bn, cont	*IMC, New York*
VOGEL, WLADIMIR	Ticinella for fl, ob, cl, sax, bn	*Suvini Zerboni*
WALTHEW, RICHARD	Triolet for trio	*Boosey & Hawkes*
WEBER, ALAIN	Sonatine for fl, bn	*Leduc*
WEBER, JOSEF M.	Septet 'Aus meinem Leben' for cl, 2hn, bn, vn, va, vc	*UE*
WELLESZ EGON	Suite for ob, cl, hn, bn Op. 73	*Sikorski*
	Octet for cl, hn, bn, str qt, cb	*Lengnick*
WESTRUP, J. A.	Divertimento for bn, vc, pf	*Augener*
ZACHOW, F. W.	Trio for fl, bn, cont	*Kistner*